DANGER RANGERS®

Poison Patrol™

Written by Sonia Sander
Illustration and Design by Rocky Hill Group and Judy O Productions, Inc.

entertain • educate • empower

E³A
educational
adventures

Educational Adventures is proud to say that this book has been approved as an excellent read-aloud storybook for young children by a leading national literacy and reading expert. Professor Linda B. Gambrell of the Eugene T. Moore School of Education at Clemson University is an author and expert in the field of reading. Among Professor Gambrell's many distinctions, she is past president of the National Reading Conference, College Reading Association and she was most recently elected to serve as president of the International Reading Association.

Produced in Association with

Safe Kids
WORLDWIDE®

This Danger Ranger's book was produced in association with Safe Kids Worldwide, a global network of organizations whose mission is to prevent accidental childhood injury, a leading killer of children 14 and under. More than 450 coalitions in 16 countries bring together health and safety experts, educators, corporations, foundations, governments and volunteers to educate and protect families. For more information on how to protect your child, please visit www.safekids.org.

entertain • educate • empower

E³A
educational
adventures

www.e3a.com

Dear Parents,

Medicine! Cleansers! Pesticides! These common household items can be toxic when safety rules go unheeded.

In this exciting story, the daring Danger Rangers go on poison patrol deliveringimportant tips on keeping children safe and avoiding serious accidents. Kids need to know when they find an open bottle of pills they should not mistake them for candy. If your child puts medicine in her mouth, it can be an emergency. Take action and call the poison control center immediately for help. Keep this important number pasted on or near the household phone and never hesitate to call for advice or information.

Since kids taking medicine by mistake is relatively common, the Danger Rangers advise storing all medications—fitted with childproof caps—away from children. Other hazardous items, such as cleansers and pesticides, should be kept locked up and out of the reach of young children as well.

The Danger Rangers also warn children to avoid toxic fumes; getting to fresh air right way is urgent if they are exposed.

Taking simple precautions can save your child from dangerous mishaps. The mighty Danger Rangers want everyone to spread the word about their safety rules on poison control.

—Alvin F. Poussaint, M.D.

Dr. Poussaint is Professor of Psychiatry at Harvard Medical School and the Judge Baker Children's Center in Boston.

Born and raised in East Harlem in a family of eight children, Dr. Poussaint graduated from Columbia University and received his M.D. from Cornell University. He then took postgraduate training at UCLA Neuropsychiatric Institute, where he served as Chief Resident in Psychiatry.

Dr. Poussaint served as a script consultant to NBC's The Cosby Show *and continues to consult to the media as an advocate of more responsible programming. He is a regular consultant for children's books, television shows and movies.*

Meet the DANGER RANGERS®

Squeeky   Burt

Sully

Burble

Kitty   Gabriela

Think Safe! Play Safe! Be Safe!

These six brave superheroes of safety are out to make the world a safer place by eliminating one danger at a time. From their top-secret headquarters, the Danger Rangers are ready to leap into action with a moment's notice.

SULLY is the team leader. He's safety-driven, smart, and funny.

KITTY is cool, smart, and adventurous; the brains of the team.

BURBLE is the team's heart and soul, the power-house and practical joker.

BURT is the very creative and part genius Personal Safety expert.

GABRIELA is the highly skilled Chief of Operations and head safety trainer.

SQUEEKY may be the smallest Danger Ranger but he also is the loudest. Good things come in small packages.

FALLBOT wants to be a Danger Ranger more than anything. As a robot he's indestructible, but that doesn't stop him from getting into more trouble than he can handle.

Fallbot

CHAPTER 1

Spic and Span Clean

At the Danger Rangers' secret headquarters, Burt was showing the team his latest invention.

"I call this my spic and span cleaner," said Burt. "This little machine will get rid of any kind of dirt—even poisons and chemicals."

"Can I try it?" asked Fallbot. "Can I? Can I?"

Before Burt could answer, Fallbot was already dangerously close to the machine.

SPLASH! Fallbot fell headfirst into the machine.

"Ow…who put that there?" he lisped.

"He'll be okay," said Burt. "It cleans metal, too."

"Great! Now, we know how to save time cleaning you after one of your falls," said Sully.

"No thanks," said Fallbot. "No thanks!"

CHAPTER 2

Babysitting Blues

Sarah loves her little brother. She likes helping her babysitter Jennie look after Luke. He needs an extra pair of eyes on him. Luke always seems to find trouble.

The day Sarah's parents cleaned and painted in the garage was no exception. They were so busy. They didn't even notice someone silently sneak into the garage. "This should do the trick," he whispered to himself as he dropped something into one of the paint cans and ran away.

Everyone was distracted that day. B–R-R-I-I-I-N-N-G-G! The phone was ringing. Jennie turned away for a moment to answer it. The call was from one of Jennie's friends. She was soon lost in conversation.

When Sarah saw that Luke had wandered off, she went looking for him.

"Luke! Luke!" called Sarah. "What are you getting into now?"

11

CHAPTER 3

Medicine Is Not Candy

SAVO SAYS:
Pills are NOT
candy.

"Oh, no! Luke, what have you got there?" cried Sarah.

Luke had found a bottle of pills. "My candy!" he screamed.

"No, Luke! That's not candy! That's medicine!" cried Sarah. "Jennie! Jennie! Help! Luke's in trouble!"

12

Jennie dropped the phone. She ran into the kitchen. Jennie quickly took the bottle away from Luke. "You can't eat that!" she said. "Taking medicine when you don't need it can hurt you. Open up, Luke. Come on, I'll trade you a cookie for what's in your mouth."

Luke opened his mouth. He spit out a pill.

SAVO SAYS: Medicine and vitamins should be locked out of reach.

13

Jennie counted all the pills to make sure there weren't any missing. "Looks like all the pills are here," she said. "That was a close call! Sarah, call the poison control center. The number is over by the phone. We need to make sure Luke is going to be okay after sucking on that pill. As soon as someone answers, hand me the phone. I need to read the label on the medicine bottle to them."

SAVO SAYS:
Call poison control immediately.

POISON HOTLINE
1-800-222-1222

CHAPTER 4

Danger Alert

Suddenly, SAVO's alarms boomed. "ALERT! ALERT! There's a poison problem at 123 Elm Street. A little boy has mistaken medicine pills for candy."

"There's not a second to lose!" called Kitty. "Prepare the hovercraft for launch immediately."

15

"That's not all Danger Rangers!" added SAVO. "Be prepared for toxic fumes, too! Sarah's parents have been painting and cleaning with some strong chemicals in the garage."

"Sounds like this house could use a serious clean sweep!" said Squeeky. "Let's go!"

CHAPTER 5

Ready to Take Charge

SAVO SAYS:
Only take medicine from an adult.

"Kitty and I will go check out the garage," Sully called out. "SAVO said that Sarah's parents were working with strong chemicals today."

Burble and the rest of the gang headed inside with Jennie and the kids.

"Taking pills is a very serious matter," said Burble. "You should only take medicine from an adult when you need it. Never, ever take medicine on your own."

17

Burble pulled Sarah and Jennie aside as Burt gave Luke a quick check-up.

"We're very proud of you two," said Burble. "You did all the right things. But I think we still have some work to do. It was too easy for Luke to get to the pills. Always make sure the childproof caps are closed tight on medicine bottles."

"Looks like Luke's one very lucky boy," said Burt. "He's going to be just fine."

"What a relief!" cried Squeeky. "How'd you two like to help us secure this place?"

"Count us in!" said Sarah and Jennie. "We don't ever want that to happen again. It was WAY too scary."

SAVO SAYS:
Cleaners should be locked out of reach.

"SAVOs on the ready and scanning," ordered Gabriela.

BEEP! BEEP! BEEP! BEEP! BEEP!

All the Danger Rangers' SAVOs were sounding their alarms. Squeeky's SAVO led him to a cabinet full of dangerou[s] cleaning products.

"This place is booby trap central!" called Squeeky. "A strong cabinet lock will solve this problem."

"You can say that again!" cried Fallbot, as bottles opened and spilled all over him.

"It's a good thing you're a robot," said Burble. "Those chemicals won't hurt you. For anyone else, a spill like that means a serious rinsing."

SAVO SAYS:
Store food and poisons separately.

"Great job team! Now nothing dangerous is being stored with the food. There's no chance for a mix up in this kitchen now!" said Gabriela. "Lets go see if Sully and Kitty need an extra hand with Sarah's parents."

CHAPTER 6

Something Smells Fishy

SAVO SAYS:
If you inhale toxic fumes, get to fresh air quickly.

Meanwhile, the strong chemicals did have an affect on Sarah's parents.

"I'm glad you Danger Rangers came and alerted us," said Sarah's mom.

"Me, too," said Sarah's dad. "We both feel so dizzy, and have headaches. I can't understand why we didn't smell the fumes."

"Breathe deep," said Kitty. "After breathing all those fumes, the fresh air is the best medicine."

"With the door open a little, we thought the garage would be well ventilated," said Sarah's dad. "Somehow we didn't smell the fumes getting stronger."

24

"The fresh air is definitely making me feel better," added Sarah's mom.
"But I still can't smell a thing."

"Smells a little fishy to me," said Squeeky. "Danger Rangers, back to the garage—
pronto!"

Burt grabbed his scanners and computer and set up shop in the garage. Burble uncovered a fingerprint. Kitty helped Burt test the paints for poisons.

"Yikes!" cried Kitty. "They've mixed different kinds of cleaners. Using cleaners and paint in a closed space is not a Danger Proof Plan! No wonder the fumes got too strong."

"We'll be able to track the bad guys once all the clues are entered into my computer," said Burt. "It looks like there's a chemical in this paint. It causes you to lose your sense of smell."

"No wonder they couldn't smell the fumes!" said Gabriela.

Paint, Chemicals

Mixing Cleaning Liquids

Loss of smell

No fresh air

Headaches, Nausea

"What did you get on the fingerprint Burble took?" asked Sully.

Just then, a skunk's mug shot popped up on Burt's computer screen.

"Looks like we're dealing with Stinky Sam," said Burt.

"Fallbot," said Sully. "We're leaving you to help Jenny's parents with the kids. Think you can handle it?"

"I'm Danger Ranger Ready," called Fallbot.

CHAPTER 7

Follow That Smell

The Danger Rangers blasted off toward Stinky Sam's factory. Gabriela hovered in the ship while the rest of the team made it down to the roof.

"Watch out," she warned. "Stinky Sam's factory looks pretty poisonous."

"You mean smells pretty poisonous, don't you, GB?" smiled Squeeky.

Once on the roof, Burble cut a hole through a skylight with his laser glasscutter. One by one the Danger Rangers headed inside.

30

"Look out!" called Burble, as he tripped over a wire. The pulled wire started a booby trap. Buckets of yellow and orange liquids poured down on them.

"Glad we have our suits, boots, and goggles on," said Kitty. "This stuff looks like it would eat right through our regular clothes!"

"We'd better be careful with this door," warned Sully. "I have a bad feeling about it. Everyone stand back."

WHOOSH! A flood of purple blasted through the open doorway.

"Burt, pal, maybe we'd better use one of your gizmos to find Stinky Sam," said Squeeky.

CHAPTER 8

No Escape

Under the protection of one of Burt's super-duper bubbles, the Danger Rangers marched on.

"My scanner has pinpointed Stinky Sam's location," said Burt. "We'll be safe from Stinky Sam's booby traps if we just follow my light."

"Whatever you do," said Kitty, "Don't touch anything until we know what we're dealing with."

"Don't forget, don't smell anything either!" added Squeeky.

"Alright team," said Sully. "We need to close off all exits. Kitty and I will head in here. Burt and Burble, you take the other door. Squeeky, I need you to drop in from above."

Stinky Sam let loose with one stinky cloud of smoke after another. He was able to hold off Kitty, Sully, Burt, and Burble. But he wasn't ready for Squeeky's sneak attack!

40   "Gotcha!" called Squeeky as he dropped a net over Stinky Sam.

CHAPTER 9

Under Arrest

"I just wanted friends," cried Stinky Sam. "I thought if everyone couldn't smell me, they'd be friends with me."

"Using poisons to trick someone into being your friend is not the way to make a friend," said Sully. "Mixing chemicals can be toxic."

Burble and Squeeky led Stinky Sam out to the police.

"It's going to be a long cleanup for those guys," said Burble.

"You mean a long, smelly cleanup," said Squeeky.

CHAPTER 10

Job Well Done

Fallbot didn't have such an easy time taking care of Luke.

But at least Luke did not get into any more trouble.

"Sarah," said Kitty. "You knew to tell an adult when you found a poison. We need more Junior Danger Rangers just like you. That's why we'd like to give you your very own SAVO."

"You mean it?" asked Sarah smiling. "I promise to be the best Junior Danger Ranger ever!"

CHAPTER II
Squeaky Clean

"I sure am glad you invented this cleaning machine when you did, Burt," said Sully.

"Me, too!" said Squeeky. "After that smelly factory today, I want to be extra squeaky clean!"

"Okay, Fallbot," said Kitty. "How about giving poison patrol a clean sweep?"

"Roger that," said Fallbot as he began to list the Poison Patrol Pointers.

"Nice work, Fallbot," said Sully. "Now I think it's time for you to get a clean sweep courtesy of Burt's new machine."

Poison Patrol Pointers

1. Pills are NOT candy.
2. Medicine and vitamins should be locked up and out of reach.
3. Call poison control (1-800-222-1222) immediately if someone has swallowed something harmful.
4. Only take medicine from adults.
5. Medicine should be in tightly closed childproof containers.
6. Store food and poisons such as medicine and cleaners separately.
7. Cleaners should be locked up and out of reach.
8. If poison spills on you, take off clothes right away and rinse well.
9. If you inhale toxic fumes, leave and get to fresh air quickly.
10. Only adults should use chemicals such as house paints and cleaners.